DRIZZLED IN MURDER

HART TIMES COZY MYSTERIES, BOOK 12

EMMA AINSLEY

SUMMER PRESCOTT BOOKS PUBLISHING

Copyright 2024 Summer Prescott Books

All Rights Reserved. No part of this publication nor any of the information herein may be quoted from, nor reproduced, in any form, including but not limited to: printing, scanning, photocopying, or any other printed, digital, or audio formats, without prior express written consent of the copyright holder.

**This book is a work of fiction. Any similarities to persons, living or dead, places of business, or situations past or present, is completely unintentional.

ONE

"Why are you smiling, Carolina?" Marissa Lopez questioned her cousin when she walked through the back door of the Hart Family Restaurant. A cool breeze blew in with her, uncommon for late summer in New Mexico.

Carolina Hart smoothed her hair with her hand as she leaned against the door jamb leading to her small office in the storage room at the back of the restaurant. She folded her arms and smiled knowingly at Marissa. "Oh, just because," she teased.

"Out with it," her uncle, Tomas Baca, known affectionately as Uncle Toad, demanded to know. He stepped away from his place at the large grill in the kitchen and cast a fatherly look in Carolina's direction. "What's going on with you?"

"Maybe I just came from the bank with some very good news," Carolina said. She turned and stepped through the door to the storage room, taking a seat at her desk.

"You came from the bank, and it was good news?" Marissa asked. "That's not usually how that happens."

"Come on, Carolina," Uncle Toad said. "We don't have all day. We're between the breakfast rush and the mid-morning rush so you might as well just admit what you're hiding from us here and now."

"Okay, it's like this," Carolina said excitedly. She had played coy for far too long. She sat forward and propped her elbows up on the desk. "Remember when we started the catering company? How I used up the rest of my savings to fund it? Well, I just checked, and not only have we made that same amount of money back, but we've doubled it." She smacked the palm of her hand on the desk for emphasis.

"Are you serious?" Marissa asked. "We've set that much money aside?"

Carolina nodded. "We have, and we're on target to triple that by the end of the year. We are doing well. No one's ready to build mansions or anything just yet, but we have come from behind."

"That's amazing news," Uncle Toad said. He stepped around the side of the desk and pulled Marissa with him. Carolina stood up and found herself wrapped in the middle of a big family hug. "Your parents would be so proud of you," Uncle Toad whispered the words in her ear as he held her.

"Thanks," Carolina said, blinking back the tears. The fact that she had lost her parents so young underscored the importance of his words. The Hart Family Restaurant itself was their dream, left in the capable hands of her uncle after they passed. Returning home to Sycamore Ridge, New Mexico after leaving her once-vibrant marketing career in Jackson Hole, Wyoming forced Carolina to think outside the box while attempting to rescue her family's business. The news from the bank meant she had been more than successful.

"Who died?" Denise Lopez, Marissa's younger sister-in-law, asked when she peered into the storage room and witnessed the group hug. "Okay, you guys are scaring me. Seriously. Who was it?"

Carolina chuckled and wiped the tears from her eyes. She shook her head and smiled. "Nobody died, Denise," she said. "We just had some very good news."

"Oh, yeah," Denise said. "I like good news. What's going on?"

"Carolina here has made a raving success out of From the Hart Catering." Uncle Toad beamed. "She just came from the bank and shared the news with us."

"Well, I wouldn't say it's a raving success," Carolina said.

"I would," Marissa said. "I was reading online that most businesses fail within the first five years. And that's before they clear a profit. So, I think we're doing well, don't you?"

Carolina nodded. "Yeah, I think we're doing alright."

DRIZZLED IN MURDER

"So, what are you going to do to celebrate?" Denise asked.

"Well, right now I'm going to help myself to cup of coffee and a seat at the table out front," Carolina said.

"You're already taking a break?" Uncle Toad complained. "You just got to work."

"I'm not taking a break," Carolina said a little sheepishly. "I'm going over our catering rates. It's quiet right now, so I'm going to sit out there with my coffee and look over our pricing list. That counts as work."

Uncle Toad grinned. "I suppose you're right," he said. "And I suppose you've earned the right to sit and sip your coffee whenever and wherever you feel like it. I'm proud of you, Carolina. I'm proud of all of you."

Carolina said nothing but patted his arm, nodding her head and choking back more tears. It was the letter he'd written to her that had played a hand in bringing her back home, and his confidence in her abilities that led her to not only revive the Hart Family Restaurant's financial outlook, but to start the catering company in the first place. No matter the details of how it happened, Uncle Toad was the reason for it all.

"Good morning," Levi said from his place in front of the prep table as Carolina passed by the kitchen. He winked at her, sending shivers down her spine.

"Good morning." Carolina smiled and rushed past the kitchen door toward the front counter. Working with her significant other could sometimes prove to be a challenge, but Levi had a way of making it fun.

With her stack of paperwork and tablet in one arm, Carolina poured the tallest mug of coffee she could find, stirred in her favorite creamer, and headed out into the dining area. She chose a booth close to the window and took a seat. She spread out her papers and turned on the tablet, then sat back and let go of a long sigh. Paperwork was never her favorite thing, but paperwork on such a positive note wasn't that bad.

Carolina reached the bottom of her coffee mug half an hour later. She looked up for a moment, eager to see something besides small numbers on a screen, and pinched the bridge of her nose. She felt a mild throb of pain behind her eyes from the strain.

"Pardon me, but I'm looking for the proprietor of the From the Hart Company," a voice called from above her. Carolina blinked her eyes open and stared at the figure standing just feet from her table. She rubbed her eyes and looked harder, making sure what her brain was telling her she was looking at was actually there.

"I'm sorry. Is this not the catering office as well?" the man said.

"Yes, it is," Carolina said, remembering her manners. She rose slightly in her seat and extended her hand to shake his. She tried her best not to stare at him. He was an older man, somewhere in his mid-sixties, she figured. But he was dressed like no other man she had ever seen before. Thin tendrils of white hair hung out from beneath his plaid beanie. He was dressed in a dark brown tweed sports coat with darker patches on the elbows. Beneath the sport coat, he wore a frilly purple shirt, fit for a role in a Shakespeare play. He topped the outfit off with a plaid kilt over stonewashed denim jeans.

The man smiled and slid into the booth across from her. "Forget my forward nature," he said. "But my name is Bronson, Bronson Declue. I'm looking to hire a catering company."

"Well, you've come to the right place," Carolina said. "What can I do for you?"

"I'm hosting a party at the Bonneville Castle," he said. "Have you heard of it? It's about twenty miles east of here, built in the 1850s in the lavish Gothic Revival architectural style. This is, by far, the most exciting venue in which I've done my work." He clapped his hands in front of his chest and grinned like an eager child awaiting their first piece of birthday cake.

"I have heard of the Bonneville Castle," Carolina said, grinning. "What sort of event are you hosting? And what can I do for you?"

"Oh, this is going to be a very exciting weekend," Bronson said. He could barely contain his giddiness. "My guests arrive late Thursday night and will remain at the castle until first thing Monday morning."

"Wow, that's a very long time to host a group of people," she said. "What are you looking for? Breakfast, lunch, and dinner? Will there be special occasions or parties? And how many guests are we looking at?"

"So many questions," Bronson said, shaking his head. "Let me do my best to answer you. I would like pastries and coffee for breakfast, sack lunches at lunchtime, informal, sit-down meals for dinner. You can bring yourself, a chef, and one other person to the castle for the weekend where you will be staying as my guest in the charming servants' quarters. I have a staff of servers who will assist you in a fully stocked kitchen. All you need to bring is yourself, your staff, and the food."

"And you said this will take place, when? A couple of weeks or so?"

Bronson's face paled, then reddened. "In two weeks? Absolutely not," he said, slapping the table for emphasis. "This weekend. This event will take place this weekend and this weekend alone. I understand this is short notice, but this is how things must go. If you can't do it, I am more than happy to check with another catering company, no hard feelings. But my question is, can you do this?"

"If there's time, absolutely we can," Carolina said cautiously. "But you see, we still have pricing to go over, food choices to discuss, and a contract to sign."

"Money is no object, let's get that out of the way first thing," Bronson said. "The menu choice is yours and yours alone, based on the requests I've already given you. And I don't care about a contract. Give me a piece of paper to sign right now and I will walk out of here and leave you all to it. You will be feeding thirty people, including yourselves and the rest of the staff. My guests and I make seven. Name your price, name your terms, whatever you want. I just want this weekend to be perfect."

"Alright then," Carolina said. "That's a lot of space you've given me. Just so we're clear, what sort of event are we speaking of? Is this a wedding? A business meeting?"

"Oh, absolutely not," Bronson said, collapsing his hands together in front of his face. "Nothing quite that pedestrian. No, this weekend is a very special event. I am hosting a murder."

Carolina choked out her agreement after a quick explanation.

DRIZZLED IN MURDER

"What does he mean, hosting a murder?" Marissa asked when Carolina returned to the storage room. She went in search of a contract template that Bronson insisted he sign before leaving the restaurant. He instructed Carolina to put in the terms later.

"He meant a murder mystery party," Uncle Toad chimed in. "At least, I hope that's what he meant."

"You nailed it, Uncle Toad," Carolina said. "Bronson is an eccentric individual who likes to go around the world hosting murder mystery parties for an eclectic group of guests. This time, he chose to host his party at the Bonneville Castle."

"Lucky us," Denise muttered.

"What are you worried about?" Marissa asked her sister-in-law. "You're not the one that has to go and deal with this."

"If you don't feel up to this, Marissa, I'm sure Denise or someone else can take your place," Carolina said. "It's a long weekend away from home. No one will think any less of you if you decide not to go with us."

"What about me?" Levi asked. "You haven't even asked me if I want to go."

"Because I already know the answer to that," Carolina said. "You wouldn't miss this for the world."

Levi smiled sheepishly. "You're right about that, sweetheart," he said, then immediately blushed from his use of the term of endearment in front of everyone else.

"It's a rush job," Carolina said, nodding her head. "But nothing we haven't done before. At least this isn't a hundred and fifty people and a bridezilla we're contending with. Although he's a little different, Bronson seems like an extremely nice man."

"You looked him up online, didn't you?" Marissa whispered.

"Of course I did," Carolina whispered back. "I wanted to make sure he was the real deal before I signed anything. I told him I was checking our calendar, but I was really checking him out."

"And he's left the door wide open for you in terms of menu," Uncle Toad said.

"Clearly, you were listening in and already know the answer, but yes, that's what he said." Carolina nodded. "I'm about to sit down with him so he can sign the contract. After that, I have a lot to do before Thursday."

"Good thing it's only Monday morning," Marissa said. "And for the record, I am coming with you. Danny can handle things." Danny Lopez, Marissa's husband, was more than capable of running the show.

"A murder mystery weekend," Denise said, shaking her head. "I'm almost jealous I can't go with you."

"I don't think this is going to be a walk in the park," Carolina said. "It's almost like catering a meal on stage during a live action performance. At least, that's what I'm trying to prepare myself for."

"You're probably in the ballpark," Uncle Toad said. "I've been to a couple of murder mystery weekends, and they are a lot of fun. But things can get crazy."

"Crazy we can handle," Levi said confidently. "As long as they don't get too out of hand."

"It's not going to be that hard of a gig," Carolina said. "He already has a waitstaff. All we have to do is prepare the food and oversee everything."

"Plus, we get to stay in that magnificent old castle for free," Marissa said.

"Sounds like I need to get back out there and get this contract signed before Bronson changes his mind," Carolina said. She left her family to work and headed back out into the dining room.

"Here you are," Bronson said a second later after he scratched his signature across the bottom of the contract. "Oh, there is one more thing." Carolina felt her heart sank. "Due to the nature of the event this weekend, you should know that cell phones will not be allowed by anyone, including staff. We don't want to give our guests any opportunity to cheat. I run a tight ship during these murder mystery weekends, and I expect my employees and contractors to do the same."

"Will there be a telephone available in case of emergencies?" Carolina asked.

"Absolutely, there will be," Bronson said, smiling reassuringly. "We even have a trained nurse on staff in case of any minor emergencies. The castle is equipped with a state-of-the-art alarm system, and, at least in the areas we will be utilizing, it is very modernized and safe."

"What about leaving our cell phones in our vehicles?" Carolina asked.

"That's not a problem at all," Bronson said, standing up from his seat. "We just don't want cell phones inside the castle. It gives the guests too many chances to figure out whodunit without relying on their instincts and problem-solving skills."

"Well, then," Carolina said. "I think we have a deal. We'll see you Thursday morning at the Bonneville Castle."

"Without your cell phones," Bronson said. He nodded his head for emphasis. "Just bring yourselves, the food, and an adventurous spirit. There will be several things that happen around the castle that will seem scary and odd to you, but I promise it's all part of the ruse. I work hard to make these weekends as real as they can get."

Carolina nodded and walked Bronson to the front door and waited while he climbed into a car and took off. It was the first time she noticed a driver had been waiting for him the entire time they met.

"Bronson had a chauffeur," she reported once he'd left.

"Seriously? Was the guy wearing a uniform and everything?" Denise asked.

"I don't know about a uniform," Carolina said. "I didn't get that close of a look. But he was wearing a funny hat."

"Oh, this weekend might just be very interesting," Marissa said.

"It gets even more interesting," Carolina said hesitantly. "We aren't allowed to take our cell phones into the castle."

"I'm sorry, what?" Marissa asked.

"I had to agree not to take our cell phones into the castle. There will be a phone on hand, but we can't take our personal phones." Carolina shifted uncomfortably on her feet.

"But what if there's an emergency with my family?" Marissa asked.

"Hey, if you don't want to go this weekend, I'll be happy to fill in for you," Denise said.

"It isn't like Bonneville Castle is that far from home, anyway," Uncle Toad said. "If anything was to happen, they can call you there or someone can

DRIZZLED IN MURDER

come knock on the front door for pity's sake. Believe it or not, there was a time when people existed without having a phone in their back pocket all the time."

"Well, I need to talk to Danny before I agree to this," Marissa said.

"Or, you could just let me go instead," Denise said.

"I would really like to go," Marissa said, glaring at her sister-in-law. "I just need to check with him first. Is that okay?"

"Of course it is," Carolina said to her cousin. She glanced at Denise. "And you are back up in case Marissa can't go. Fair enough?"

"Yeah, fair enough," Denise said.

"Why don't they want us to take our cell phones?" Levi asked.

"Oh, that's easy," Uncle Toad said. "They don't want anyone cheating."

"How do you cheat at a murder mystery weekend?" Levi asked.

Carolina hadn't thought to ask the same question. "I'm not sure."

"How many storylines do you think these murder mystery weekend games have?" Uncle Toad asked. "I'm sure Mr. Declue only wants people there who won't look up any way to cheat. That's all."

"You're probably right, Uncle Toad," Carolina said. "But if this is going to be a deal breaker, I will simply call him and tell him we can't do it.

"Right," he said. "I'm sure Jocelyn Hendricks would love to take over for us."

"Not a chance," she huffed. There was no way her business rival was going to get anywhere near this job.

TWO

Carolina eased the catering van slowly down the narrow driveway. Both sides were surrounded by pine trees packed densely together and looming high above, casting an eerie shadow over them as they drove. It was early morning, just before dawn, and the van was packed full of food for the weekend.

As a child, nearly every resident within one hundred miles of Bonneville Castle took a field trip there before the end of elementary school. Carolina was no exception, but when the castle came into view as they neared the end of the driveway, she felt her heart begin to race. Typically, things seen in childhood appeared smaller and less significant as an adult. The opposite was true for Bonneville Castle.

Maybe it was the effect of the dim, early morning light, but the tall spires and gothic windows seemed a little sinister to her.

"How many rooms does this place have again?" Marissa asked when Carolina followed the driveway around the right side of the structure. Bronson had given her specific directions to pull around to the back of the castle. For a moment, she felt like they would never reach their destination given how large the place was.

"I'm trying to remember from fourth grade when we came here as a class," Carolina said. "It seems like there's more than eighty rooms, or something like that."

"You visited here as a kid?" Levi asked, not taking his eyes off the castle. "I would have been scared out of my skin."

"For some reason, it didn't seem as big when I was a kid," Carolina said.

"I was thinking that same thing," Marissa mumbled.

Carolina wondered if she was beginning to regret her decision to accompany them on the weekend

DRIZZLED IN MURDER

catering gig instead of letting her sister-in-law take over.

"This place is like four stories tall," Levi said.

"And that's not including the basement and the sub-basement," Carolina said.

"There's a basement beneath the basement?" Marissa asked.

Caroline nodded. "That's what the website said."

"I don't think I've ever seen such a big place," Levi said.

"And this Bronson guy, he owns this?" Marissa asked.

"No, Bronson isn't the owner," Carolina said. "He's the coordinator for this weekend. I guess he goes all over the world and hosts these murder mystery weekends."

"Does somebody actually live here?" Marissa asked.

"Yeah, someone does," Carolina said. "The owner is a retired university professor named Tobin Crutch-field. From what I was reading, he's a bit of an eccentric guy."

"You don't say," Levi said sarcastically.

"Does he have a family? Does he live in this place all by himself?" Marissa shook her head slowly and continued to gaze up at the side of the steep structure.

"I don't know," Carolina said. "I'd think it would become lonely to live in such a big place by yourself, though."

"You could house a small community here," Levi said.

Carolina said nothing more. She was too busy trying to find the covered doorway Bronson had described to her in his instructions. She eased the catering van over the pebble stone driveway until they were behind the center of the building. She stopped in front of a small area that appeared to have been added sometime after the original construction. Unlike the rest of the castle, the addition appeared to be constructed of masonry brick, painted a deep gray to match the rest of the castle.

"I think this is it," she said, pointing to a door tucked into a small alcove. "Bronson said I'd know the entrance to the kitchen because it wouldn't match the rest of the castle."

"What are we supposed to do? Just knock?" Levi asked. He waited while Carolina parked the van, then opened the passenger door and stepped out.

Before she could answer, the door swung open. Bronson emerged, dressed this time in a yellow raincoat, red basketball shorts, and a pair of flip flops. "You made it," he said. "Come on in and I will show you around."

"We have a bunch of food we need to get inside," Carolina protested. "Most of it is perishable."

"Nonsense. My staff will come and take care of that for you," Bronson said. He hooked Carolina's arm in his own. "I already told you the only thing you have to worry about this weekend is preparing these wonderful meals you have planned for us."

"The rest of us can help," Levi said. Carolina glanced over her shoulder at him. He stood tall, with his arms at his sides and his shoulders back. It was his protective stance.

"I think we're okay, Levi," Carolina said. She willed him to read her mind. She had no concerns over

Bronson Declue and his intentions. He was eccentric, that much was true, but she figured he was harmless.

"When do we serve for the first time?" Marissa asked.

"We have appetizers prepared for cocktails this evening," Carolina informed her.

"You have appetizers for us? That's just splendid," Bronson said, grinning ear to ear and beaming at Carolina.

"You mentioned the cocktail hour and appetizers this evening," Carolina said. "I just assumed you meant you wanted us to prepare the hors d'oeuvres."

"The conversation I remember back at the Hart Family Restaurant consisted of pastries and coffees for breakfast, bagged meals for lunches, and a nice, sit-down meal for dinner," Bronson said. He paused just inside the entrance. "The fact that you took the additional step to prepare appetizers for us this evening is wonderful. I certainly did not expect that."

"Which way should we go?" Levi asked. His face had grown sullen.

"Right this way," Bronson said. He turned right but moved quickly when a line of uniformed staff members filed past him like soldiers marching to war. Each was dressed the same from head to toe. A black ball cap pulled low over their eyes, red collared shirt, and black pants with a black apron tied around their waists.

"Who are they?" Marissa asked.

"They are my staff," Bronson said casually. "They go everywhere with me. Trust me, this is all in a day's work for them. They will have your food tucked away in no time. Meanwhile, let me show you around."

They continued down the hallway until Bronson led them through the wide, arched doorway into a cavernous room. The room itself was a circular shape with the largest fireplace Carolina had ever seen at the far end. Two other arch entryways flanked them on the left and right. She was surprised to see three cast iron stoves standing in various places around the room. She was relieved when she turned around and spotted two stainless-steel, six-burner professional stoves. At least they wouldn't have to cook like they were in medieval times, she thought.

In the center of the room, three long butcher block counters stood with just enough room in between for two people to stand back-to-back. "This is the prep area," Bronson explained. "You will find absolutely everything you need in the small cupboards."

"Where is the pantry?" Carolina asked. She turned in a complete circle and faced the door they had just walked through. Two large refrigerators stood on either side of the entryway.

He held up a finger. "Our host, Tobin, supplied his staff with state-of-the-art appliances rather than altering the interior of his historical home by installing a walk-in cooler. He found these commercial refrigerators to be the next best thing. You will find your perishables stocked in each refrigerator for your convenience," Bronson said. He led them through the kitchen and under the archway to the left of the massive fireplace. They turned down a narrow, dimly lit hallway.

"Watch your step," Bronson instructed. Carolina was surprised to see a narrow staircase open up beneath them.

"Wow," Marissa said. "Someone could get really hurt if they didn't know to look for stairs here."

"Indeed," Bronson said quietly. "This is the reason I always tour every venue before I ask my staff to join me. I nearly fell down these steps myself the first time."

"I suppose it's a good thing you're taking us through now yourself, then," Levi said.

"Can you imagine the lawsuit if I didn't?" Bronson said with a chuckle.

"Where are we going?" Carolina asked when the stairs wound around for the third time.

"To your pantry," Bronson said, stopping in the middle of the narrow staircase. "You will find in these old castles; the pantry was kept in the basement below the kitchen. Back then it was called a larder, and staff members took advantage of cooler temperatures underground. Of course, nowadays we have those massive industrial refrigerators to keep things fresh, but extra supplies are still stored downstairs."

He led them through another narrow hall at the bottom of the steps. Instead of ornate arched doorways, the entryway was simply a gap between large concrete walls. Bronson flipped on the lights and revealed the largest storeroom Carolina had ever seen. Wire shelves filled the center of the room, roughly the size of the kitchen above it. But the walls were still lined with the old-fashioned wooden shelves she imagined had come with the construction of the castle.

"Did your staff put any of our things down here?" Levi asked.

Bronson nodded. "For your convenience, your items have been placed to your right, just inside the doorway." He motioned toward three large shelving units, the only shelves in the entire space that appeared to have been recently dusted.

"I'm not sure if I'd call that convenient," Marissa admitted.

"Oh, but it will be," Bronson said brightly. "As I stated before, you will have my staff at your disposal. You just tell them what you want, and they will run down the steps and fetch it for you. It's really that simple." He turned and headed back through the doorway toward the hall, flipping the lights off as he went.

"Now where are we going?" Marissa muttered under her breath.

"Up the stairs, my dear," Bronson said.

"Please tell me this is the end of the stairs," Levi said.

"Technically, it's not," Bronson said as he walked ahead of them. "However, Tobin had the foresight to install a set of elevators between the main floor and the Great Hall above."

"It's too bad he didn't install one between the kitchen and the pantry," Carolina said.

Her comment earned a knowing look from Bronson. He turned around mid-step and rolled his eyes. "That's exactly what my staff members said on their first tour as well," he said. "I can't say I don't agree with them."

They passed the first arched entryway to the kitchen and continued down a wide hallway. By Carolina's calculations, they were on the far side of the addition behind the castle. She spotted the silver elevator doors and found herself gasping to catch her breath when the doors opened on the second floor. She had seen the room before as a child but hadn't quite remembered a room so grand and ornate.

They stood at the back, gazing at the extra-high ceilings covered with a grid of dark wood. A smaller grid covered the wall below from the floor up to shoulder height on the men. Above that, the walls were painted a deep red, giving the space an ancient vibe. The room was long and wide, though the length was easily twice the width. At the far end, she could see a long table that seated a dozen people. There were no chairs on the opposite side, allowing guests to look forward at the other tables that dotted the Great Hall.

"This place is huge," Marissa said.

"I'm sure you're wondering where you will be sleeping," Bronson said. He headed toward the far end of the room and out a door into a large hallway. The hallway was nearly as ornate as the hall had been. The same woodwork that lined the walls in there, continued down the hallway. After they walked what felt like the length of three football fields, they reached the end. Bronson stepped forward and pushed through a set of double doors. The doors opened into a wide, sunny sitting room. Large windows covered the exterior wall.

"What is this place?" Marissa asked, stepping inside. She ran her hand over a powder blue settee.

"Your quarters," Bronson said proudly. "I had planned to place you in the servants' quarters behind the kitchen, but Tobin just insisted you occupy this guest chamber instead. Behind each of those doors is a bedroom with its own washroom. I will leave you to it."

"Where are our things?" Carolina asked.

"Already delivered to your rooms," Bronson said, smiling proudly. "My staff is very efficient, you will find." He turned on his heel.

"What time do we need to begin preparations for dinner?" Carolina asked before he left.

"An informal dinner will be served at five," he said. "But remember, you will not be preparing dinner tonight. You will be served as guests. However, appetizers you're providing will need to be served promptly at eight."

Carolina glanced at Levi who nodded his head. "That works just fine," Carolina said. "I assume we are to remain here in the meantime?"

"You are welcome to explore the corridor outside," Bronson said. "You will find a library, other bed chambers, and a few sitting rooms. But please, do not venture beyond the hallway." He opened the double doors again and exited with gusto.

"I'm not sure which one is stranger," Levi muttered as soon as he was gone. "This place or the man that brought us here."

THREE

Carolina checked her reflection in the mirror before she left her room within the walls of Bonneville Castle. She shook her head in disbelief when she walked into the adjoining lounge where Levi and Marissa were waiting for her.

"Who would have thought that we'd be catering a murder mystery weekend in this place?" she asked, shaking her head.

"Who would have thought we'd be fixing hors d'oeuvres in the kitchen of a gothic castle," Levi said. He opened the wooden double doors for Carolina and Marissa and led them into the corridor. When they reached the kitchen, Carolina pointed to three covered plates set on the large table in the butcher block counter in the center of the kitchen. As soon as she walked through the arched doorway, she was met with savory aromas.

"Something smells good," Marissa said. She rushed ahead of them and uncovered one of the plates.

"Chicken pot pie," Levi announced, gazing at the plate.

"Yeah, with smashed potatoes and sourdough rolls," Marissa said. She pulled a wooden stool out from under the counter and took a seat. Levi and Carolina followed suit. She plunged her fork into the golden-brown crust and took a bite.

"Oh, that's divine," she said, closing her eyes. They ate quickly, savoring the wonderful food. As soon as dinner was over, they placed their plates in the large dishwasher and got to work on the appetizers for cocktail hour.

"Isn't it weird that we're making appetizers following dinner?" Marissa asked.

"Not necessarily," Carolina said. "Bronson said the guests would arrive later this evening. Dinner was just for us, not them."

"I hadn't thought of that," Marissa said. She turned her attention back to the phyllo dough she painstakingly unrolled at the counter. She cut each pastry sheet into six pieces and passed them down the counter to Carolina, who carefully wrapped them around a large square of feta cheese. Carolina then placed each of the squares on a greased baking sheet and transported the pan to the oven.

As soon as the feta cheese appetizers were ready, Carolina drizzled warm honey over the top and lightly rolled them in sesame seeds. Meanwhile, Levi assembled an array of olives, stuffed grape leaves, mini cucumber slices, fresh celery sticks, hard Greek cheeses, and artichoke hearts on carved wood platters. He spooned his own spicy hummus dip into bowls and placed them on several other trays alongside toasted mini baguettes and fresh pita chips.

"I see you went with a Mediterranean theme for the evening," Bronson said when they handed the appetizer trays off to his waiting staff members. "Please, follow me upstairs to the Great Hall. I would like for you to meet some of my guests for the weekend."

Carolina nodded, though she considered the request a bit unusual. She had assumed that the addition of over a dozen staff members meant that Bronson intended for the catering staff to stay hidden from the guests. Still, she followed behind him down the narrow hall to the waiting elevator.

Her breath was taken from her for a second time the moment the elevator doors opened to the massive hall. She spotted the guests clumped together, carrying on lively conversations. A mobile bar had appeared in the corner of the room near the end of the banquet table in front. Two of Bronson's staff members, still dressed in red shirts and black pants, moved quickly behind the stainless-steel counter.

A line of eight staff members placed the appetizer trays precisely in the center of the long banquet table. Bronson stood in the middle of the room and clapped his hands together suddenly. "Ladies and gentlemen," he said. "I would like for you to avail yourselves to the fresh appetizers supplied for us tonight by From the Hart Catering. Here are the principals of the company. Let's give them a round of applause for what promises to be a decadent weekend, in more ways than one."

Carolina stood next to Marissa, unsure what to do with herself as the group trained their focus on the three of them, clapping politely. She hoped Bronson would quickly dismiss them to return to the kitchen, and then to their quarters.

Instead, he insisted upon introducing each of his guests, one by one. First up was Tobin Crutchfield, a small, gray-haired man who was the owner the enormous Bonneville Castle. Delana Murtaugh was next, a small-boned woman with black hair and ivory skin. Bronson described her as the owner of several small boutiques along the New England coast, though she quickly corrected him and pronounced herself a fashion industry titan.

Next was Darien Chambers, Delana's sullen younger brother and an unemployed actor. He scowled at Bronson as he spoke about his limited resume. A tall, regal man was next, whom Bronson described as a renowned stage actor known for his performances on London stages. Simon Ambrose averted his eyes toward the ceiling the entire time Bronson described his biography.

Last he introduced Larry Smith, a wealthy Texas rancher, and Coy Caulfield, a large man with broad shoulders and a trick knee leftover from his days as a professional football player. Coy smiled congenially at each of them. Larry nodded his head, but the rest of the guests essentially ignored them once the introductions were over.

"How does this whole thing work exactly?" the rancher asked Bronson a moment later. "I mean, I get the basic premise. Even a dumb old country boy like me understands what a murder mystery is all about. I just don't get the logistics of it all." He laughed heartily for a moment, but quieted quickly once it was apparent than none of the other guests intended to laugh with him.

"It is really quite simple," Simon said with exaggerated empathy. "One of us will be the victim, and another one of us is the murderer. The rest of us are tasked with figuring out who is who by the end of weekend."

"Do those people already know who they are?" Coy asked. "Or do we draw names or something?"

Bronson stepped between them, shaking his head. "The roles have already been established," he said. "Which means if you don't already know that you have been picked to fill one of those roles, you are going to solve the crime."

The room fell silent for a moment. Darien cleared his throat and turned to Bronson. "Is there a reason the catering staff is still in here with the rest of us?" he asked, scowling at Levi and Marissa.

"Oh, well, I just wanted to introduce all of you to our very capable caterers," Bronson said, evidently taken aback by the bluntness of the question. "Carolina is the owner of a restaurant in Sycamore Ridge, a wonderful city not far from Bonneville Castle."

Darien turned his attention away from Bronson as he spoke. Their eccentric host sighed deeply and slumped for a moment at the obvious snub from one of his guests. Carolina instantly felt bad for him.

"Why don't the three of us find our way back to the kitchen?" she suggested to Levi and Marissa.

"Why don't I walk you all back to the elevator," Bronson said quietly after Carolina spoke. He turned to glare at Darien's back before he followed them toward the far side of the great hall.

Carolina glanced at the guests one last time before she turned to follow Marissa and Levi. Delana and Darien had their heads bent together in a vigorous conversation. She wondered if the older sister was chastising her younger brother for his atrocious behavior. Simon, Larry, and Coy stood close to the bar, each with a small glass in their hands, halfway filled with amber-colored whiskey. Tobin stood close to the edge of the buffet table with his arms folded over his chest.

"I think he was scowling," she told Marissa and Levi a few moments later in their shared lounge.

"You think?" Levi asked mildly.

"No, I'm quite sure it was a scowl," Carolina said. She eased herself into one of the large, oversized chairs. "Wow, this is so comfortable."

Marissa followed her example and took a seat across the small sitting area from her. "Why do you think he was scowling?" she asked.

"I don't know." Carolina rested her head against the back of the chair and closed her eyes.

"Maybe he's not too excited about this weekend."

"Then why would he have agreed to have it here?" Levi asked. He settled into another chair.

"Maybe he needs the money," Marissa said. "It can't be cheap, owning a place like this."

"I think you're onto something," Carolina said, raising her head for a moment. "He lives here alone, and he probably gets quite a tidy sum out of being the venue for this event."

The conversation died off, and Carolina felt herself slipping easily into a nap. She woke once but closed her eyes again when she heard Marissa's soft snoring. Levi's head was back as well, and his eyes were closed.

Carolina woke with a start two hours after she eased into the large chair. The room had dimmed considerably as the evening wore on. At first, she didn't recognize her uncomfortable surroundings. She was jolted a second time by a loud and shrill screech.

Levi jumped to his feet. "What was that?"

"I don't know," Carolina said. She got up and moved slowly along the wall behind her, feeling for a light switch. When she found one, she quickly pushed it up. Three lamps immediately illuminated. Marissa remained sound asleep.

Another screech filled the room. Marissa opened her eyes suddenly and jumped to her feet. "What's going on?" she asked.

"I think it's coming from down the corridor," Carolina said. She pushed the chair out of her way and headed toward the door.

"Wait a minute," Levi said, moving quickly to intercept her. "We don't know what's going on out there."

"We know something is going on," Carolina said.

"Yeah, but that doesn't mean we have to go and see what it is," Marissa said. She stood close to one of the large windows until a bright flash of lightning followed by a peal of thunder that rattled the glass sent her scampering toward Carolina and Levi.

"What a storm," she said, gripping Carolina's arm tightly. "I didn't expect that."

The sound of footsteps filled the hall. Carolina waited by the door for a moment, listening. She could hear three or four sets of footsteps. She placed her hands on the doorknob and began to twist it open but hesitated when another loud peal of thunder boomed outside followed by a new round of lightning.

More screams followed when the lights went down, plunging the large estate into complete darkness. "Now what?" Marissa cried softly.

"Now we go check out what's going on," Carolina said. "And we stick together." She eased the door open slowly. Levi stood close behind her; she could feel his breath on the back of her neck as she stepped cautiously out into the hallway.

"Stay close," she heard him say to Marissa who took up the rear behind him.

"I think it came from the other end of the hall," Carolina whispered.

"I think so, too," Levi said, guiding her toward the direction of the corridor opposite the kitchen.

Slowly, they walked about twenty steps before more voices reached them. Carolina stopped suddenly and reached back to grip Levi's arm, communicating her desire to wait and listen for a moment before moving further.

"Hello," a male voice called out. "Who's there?" A narrow shaft of light from a flashlight danced up and down the corridor walls.

"It's Carolina, Levi, and Marissa," she called back. "We're the caterers. Who is this?"

"Larry Smith," the rancher called back. "I'm down here in the library."

Carolina took his comments as an invitation to advance toward his location. She felt along the wall for the decorative wooden rail. Levi and Marissa moved behind her. They walked for another minute before the flashlight beam found them.

"We're in here," Larry said. "I'm afraid that something bad has happened." Carolina moved under the large door frame. She could see tall shelves of books towering over the room in the beams from the other flashlights. She scanned the others as quickly as the light allowed. Simon stood directly behind Larry, Tobin was directly on his left, and Delana was on his right, hugging herself tightly and hanging her head.

"Carolina," Levi whispered behind her. He placed his hand gently on the back of her neck and guided her to look down. There on the floor, Bronson Declue lay before her, his face illuminated by the beam from Larry's flashlight. His eyes were open and gazing toward something on the other side of the room.

"What's going on?" she asked. "What is he looking at?"

"Carolina," Levi said quietly. "He isn't looking at anything. I'm afraid he's dead."

FOUR

"The storm knocked out the power," Tobin announced a moment later. "I'm afraid we're locked inside the castle until the power returns or help arrives."

"What do you mean, we're locked in here?" Larry demanded, raising his flashlight to Tobin's face.

"Please put that down and don't shine it in my eyes," Tobin said. "It's just as I said. There is a failsafe built into the security system that prevents the doors from opening if there is a power outage."

"But why?" Delana whined. "Why would you put that into your security system in the first place? What if there was a fire?"

"The point was to prevent burglars from cutting the power and gaining access to the castle," Tobin said. "But I can see the error in that plan now that we're standing here in the dark."

"Where is the phone?" Carolina asked.

"What phone?" Tobin asked.

"The landline," Carolina said. "Bronson said we had to leave our cell phones behind but assured me that there was a phone available in case of an emergency."

"I'm afraid Bronson was mistaken," Tobin said. "I have no phone lines, no internet service. I wanted this place to be as rustic and traditional as possible."

"So how do we get help?" Marissa asked.

"We don't," Tobin said. "Not until the power comes back on, anyway."

"I can't remember the last time we had a major storm like this here," Carolina said.

"What are we supposed to do now?" Delana asked.

"People, people," Simon said. He held his flashlight close to his face, casting shadows on his eyes and giving him an eerie appearance. "I can't believe I have to say this, but don't you see what's going on here? This is all a part of the game. Only I'm shocked that he involved the caterers in the ruse, no offense to all of you."

"What are you talking about?" Delana asked. "Bronson is dead."

"No, he's not," Simon said. "He's acting. Maybe my trained eye simply knows what to see before the average human, but he is clearly putting on a show."

"I don't think so, bud," Larry said, shining his flashlight over Bronson's body again.

Carolina knelt beside Bronson's body. She gently felt for his arm and rolled his sleeve up to expose his wrist. She pressed her fingers into the skin below his thumb and waited. "I don't feel anything," she announced, looking up.

Larry moved to his knees. He held the flashlight under his armpit and reached his free hand under Bronson's neck. He felt around for a moment, then sighed deeply. "I'm afraid not, partner," he said, looking up at Simon. "This man doesn't have a pulse. He's deader than a doornail. The best I can see, he's got a mighty big gash on the back of his head." He shone his light on the floor around Bronson's body and stopped when the beam reached a glass candle holder.

"Look, we have to get out of here," Levi said suddenly. "As soon as this storm is over, someone needs to go to the ground floor and break a window. Our vehicle is still in the back. We can get out of here and go get help."

"I'm afraid that won't work either," Tobin said.

"What do you mean, it won't work?" Larry demanded. "Are you telling me we can't break these windows? That's the most absurd thing I've ever heard."

"I'm telling you that it won't work," Tobin said. "Most of you haven't gotten a good look at the windows from the outside of the castle. If you break a window from this height and attempt to get out, you will never make it to the ground. You'll break your neck before you get there."

"Okay, but what about the bottom level?" Carolina asked. "What about the entryway we came through when we arrived at the back of the castle? Surely we can make it out that way."

Tobin shook his head. It was difficult to see his features in the darkness. "I'm afraid that way is out, too," he said. "What you may not have noticed on the windows at ground level is a sophisticated, metal net-mesh woven into the glass. The windows are unbreakable."

"Okay, then, where is your fire exit?" Simon asked. His London accent faded slightly. "This is the U.S. Surely a large castle like this has some legal requirement to have a clearly marked fire exit. How are you supposed to get out of here if the structure catches on fire?"

"I'm afraid there's nothing we can do," Tobin said. "I was in the process of updating fire escape hatches surrounding the property, but none of them have been completed yet."

"This sure sounds convenient to me," Larry said.

"What is that supposed to mean?" Tobin asked.

"It sure seems to me like you have all the answers for why we can't get out of this place," Larry said.

"What are you implying, Mr. Smith?" Tobin asked.

"I'm not implying anything," Larry said. "I'm simply saying that it sure seems like a deliberate attempt to keep all of us trapped here. Of course, unless Simon is right, and you're just part of some elaborate ruse."

"I can assure you, this is not part of the murder mystery weekend," Tobin said.

"Yeah, but how do we know that?" Marissa said.

"For one thing, I know who was supposed to be the victim," Tobin said.

"You do?" Simon asked doubtfully. "Were you in on the script or something?"

"I was, actually," Tobin said. "It's something Bronson and I worked on before any of you arrived, including the caterers."

"What you're trying to say is none of this was part of the script?" Delana asked.

"That's exactly what I'm trying to tell you," Tobin said. "Someone murdered this man. I don't know who it was or why they did it, but none of this is part of the weekend. For one thing, no one was really supposed to die."

DRIZZLED IN MURDER

"And the power outage? Was that part of it?" Levi asked.

"Absolutely not," Tobin said. "Think about it. Wouldn't we have requested a specific menu from you if we had planned a power outage? Or, at least, provided some way for you to still cook for the rest of us?"

"How long do you suppose the lights will stay out?" Delana asked.

"I really don't have any good way of knowing that," Tobin said.

"Have they gone out before?" Carolina asked.

"Never," Tobin said. "Not like this, anyway. Remember, thunderstorms like this are extremely rare in this part of New Mexico."

"What are we supposed to do now?" Delana cried again. "We can't just leave a dead man here in the middle of the library. Not to mention, there's a killer on the loose in this castle."

"And it might be any one of us," Larry said.

"He's got a point," Simon said. "It might be any one of us or the rest of us who aren't here."

53

"It could be one of them," Delana said, pointing to Levi, Carolina, and Marissa.

"Doubtful," Tobin said. "The three of them were in their chambers before the lights went out. They didn't even know where the library was."

"That doesn't prove anything," Delana said.

"It does cast a lot of doubt on them as suspects," Larry said. "This place is so large; how would they have gotten all this way without the rest of us hearing them?"

"Good point," Simon said. "I guess that means we can eliminate the catering staff as murderers."

"Is that what we're doing now? Trying to solve a murder, only this time for real?" Delana complained.

"Do you have a better idea?" Larry pushed back. "Because right now, finding out who killed this man is probably our best option."

"I disagree," Simon said. "Our best option is to get somewhere where there's light and where we can keep an eye on each other."

"Where do you suggest we go, then?" Carolina asked.

DRIZZLED IN MURDER

"To the Great Hall," Tobin said. "There are candles there that can be lit. We need to find the others as well."

"But what about food?" Levi said. "The Great Hall is one story above the kitchen."

"All the better," Tobin said. "There's a single staircase that leads down to the kitchen. It will be much harder to get separated and lost if we are just going to and from."

"Let's say all of us move together toward the Great Hall," Larry said. "What about him? What do we do with the body?"

"Unless you men plan on carrying him up and down the stairs, I suppose our best bet is to leave him where he is," Tobin said. "Besides, when the cops are able to arrive, they're going to want to see the crime scene as undisturbed as possible."

"I've got to hand it to you, Mr. Crutchfield," Larry said. "You're either a very calm thinker who is good in a crisis, or very, very calculating and conniving."

"Let's just hope it's the former," Simon said.

FIVE

Reluctantly, Carolina hooked her arm around Levi's and reached back for Marissa's hand as the group started toward the exit of the library. Tobin led the way with his flashlight shining as far ahead down the corridor as possible. Delana walked behind him, muttering and complaining as she walked. Carolina, Marissa, and Levi were next, followed by Simon and Larry.

"I suppose it's a good thing we're on the same floor as the Great Hall," Simon commented from behind. "I would hate to try to traverse the steps with nothing more than a few flashlight beams to light the way."

Before anyone could answer, thunder shook the windows on the exterior of the castle once again. Lightning flashed, briefly illuminating the hall in a few areas, revealing open doorways. The group walked past the bed chambers where Carolina and her crew had been placed. The broad corridor took on a sinister feel in the darkness. Carolina held tightly to her cousin and Levi as she walked.

"Hello, is anyone there?" a voice called in the distance. "Anyone? The lights are out, and I don't know where I'm at."

Carolina thought she recognized the voice of Coy Caulfield, the former professional football player. She waited for someone to call back to him. "Aren't you going to answer him?" she asked Tobin a moment later.

"I was hoping to get a better idea of where he might be first," Tobin said.

"Hello, is anyone there?" Coy called out again.

"We're here," Tobin said. "In the east corridor headed toward the Great Hall. If you can find it, meet us there."

"I'm in the Great Hall," Coy said. "Who else is with you?"

"We'll explain when we get there," Tobin said. "Are you alone?"

There was a break in the conversation. Carolina could hear something in the distance, something like feet shuffling down the hallway. She felt the blood in her veins turn to ice. Someone was close, she could sense it. But when Coy called out again at last, his voice appeared to be in the same place it had been before.

"Yeah, I'm alone," Coy said at last. "I think I'm in the middle of the room. I wish I had my phone, then I could have a flashlight."

"We have flashlights," Tobin said. Carolina sensed they were close to the entryway.

"I thought you said there were candles," Simon asked.

"There are," Tobin said. "But I don't want him to go searching for them and lose sense of where he's at. Besides, it would be difficult to light a match in the darkness without starting a fire. I know what I'm doing."

"I'm sure you do," Larry muttered behind Carolina. She wondered if anyone else heard his words.

"We're just now entering the Great Hall," Tobin called out. He stopped walking and shone his flashlight to the left and then to the right.

"I see the light," Coy said. "I'm coming to you."

There was a great crash and a groan. Carolina stopped walking and clung tightly to Levi. "Are you alright?" Tobin called out.

"Yeah, fine," Coy whispered. "I think I found the end of the table."

"Which one?" Tobin asked. "This space is filled with tables."

"That great big, long one at the front of the room," Coy said, his voice returning.

"Stay where you are," Tobin ordered. His flashlight beam found the high-backed chairs that were pushed under the long table in the front. Carolina saw him place his hand on the back of the chair closest to him. He followed the line of chairs down toward the end on the left. Delana fell in step behind him, followed by everyone else.

DRIZZLED IN MURDER

"Oh, man, am I glad to see you," Coy said. Carolina can see his face illuminated in the flashlight beam. "Who is with you?"

"Delana. I'm here," she said.

"So are we. Carolina, Marissa, and Levi, the caterers," Carolina said next.

"Simon Ambrose here," Simon said.

"Larry Smith," Larry said.

"What about Darien?" Delana asked. "Where is my brother?"

"Where is Bronson, you know, the host dude?" Coy asked.

"I'm afraid we have some bad news about Bronson," Tobin said. "Why don't we find our way to the center of the room, and I can light a few candles."

"What about Bronson?" Coy asked. "Where is he?"

"I'm afraid he's lying on the floor of the library, dead," Tobin said. His voice seemed devoid of any emotion.

"Dead? What do you mean, he's dead?" Coy asked.

"As I said before, let's head toward the center of the room where we can light a few candles," Tobin said.

"Oh, no. No, no," Coy said. Carolina could see the wave of his hand in the dim light. "I'm not moving until I hear more answers. What do you mean he's dead?"

"Just what he said, I'm afraid," Larry said. "He's not lying, and before you ask, this is not part of the murder mystery weekend game."

There was silence for a moment. Carolina could hear Coy's deep inhaling and exhaling as he processed the information. "You're for real, aren't you?"

"He's right," Carolina said. "I checked him myself. So did Larry."

"So, then, that means," Coy said slowly. "We have a killer on our hands."

"It would appear so," Tobin said. His flashlight began to move again, headed toward the middle of the room. They each followed him, single file this time, as he wove his way around the tables and through the chairs. He stopped and set his flashlight down on a grand sideboard next to the ornate wall.

62

They listened intently as Tobin went to work opening and closing several drawers and cabinets. A moment later, he struck a match and began lighting several candles at once.

When he was finished, light danced around them. She counted four large candelabras, each filled with half a dozen tall candles. Tobin reached for the first candelabra and turned around, handing it off to Levi.

"Walk straight across to the far side of the room. You'll find another set of candelabras," Tobin said. "Take one of the candles and light it."

He reached for the second candelabra, passing it to Larry, and giving him similar instructions. "Find your way carefully to the long end, close to the entryway that leads to the steps going downstairs to the kitchen," he instructed. "Again, you will find several other candelabras. Light them."

Soon, the cavernous hall was filled with an eerie glowing light from the candles. Carolina felt a slight sense of relief. She could see everyone in the room with her for the first time since the lights went out. They gathered in the center, carefully placing their candles on the round tables close to them.

"Now what?" Delana asked. "Who's going to go look for my brother?"

"I don't think anyone needs to go look for anybody," Simon said. "Our best bet is to stick together."

"Well, someone has to find my brother," Delana said, her voice raising. "It isn't fair that he's stuck out there in the darkness all alone."

"I think he's correct," Tobin said. "Our best bet is to remain here together."

"But what about Darien?" Delana cried out loudly. "Like you said, there's a killer out there."

"If we're all in here together," Larry said. "Your brother should be safe out there alone. That means, unless he's the killer, the killer is in here with us."

"Are you accusing my brother of killing Bronson?" Delana balled her fists and stepped closer to the rancher. "Because if you are, you're going to have to take that back."

"I'm not accusing anyone," Larry said. "I'm just pointing out that unless it was your brother, the killer is most likely in here with us."

"Not so fast," Carolina said. "You seem to be forgetting more than a dozen staff members Bronson brought with him. Where are they? And how are they getting along?"

"Oh, my goodness," Tobin said. "I forgot all about them. They were in the garret, in the servants' quarters up there."

"The garret? Where is that?" Delana asked.

"Top floor," Tobin said. "In the attic. That's the traditional place where servants used to sleep. There's plenty of room there."

"Are you sure that's where they all went?" Carolina asked. "I hate to think of them wandering around the castle in the dark."

"That's where they were supposed to go," Tobin said. "Although, I can't say for sure that's where they are."

"Maybe your brother is with them," Marissa suggested.

"With the servants? What are you insinuating?" Delana asked.

"I'm not insinuating a thing," Marissa said. "I was just suggesting that maybe your brother found the company of Bronson's staff members. That's all. That would mean he's not wandering around alone in the dark."

"It sounds to me like you're saying he belongs with the servants," Delana said.

"How did you get that from what I said?" Marissa asked.

Carolina felt a chill go down her back. Less than an hour into the situation, and they were already unraveling. She squeezed Marissa's hand and cleared her throat. "I think we need to calm down a bit," she said. "Delana, maybe you need to dial back on getting offended about your brother. I think the last thing any of us want to do right now is insult you or him."

"I don't take kindly to being put down, and I certainly don't put up with anyone insulting members of my family," Delana said through gritted teeth.

"Surely you can appreciate the fact that we're all in a high stress environment at the moment," Simon said. "Nobody meant to insult anyone. Do you understand that?"

DRIZZLED IN MURDER

Carolina stiffened, prepared for the verbal war she expected to break out after Simon's comments. But she was surprised to see Delana pull out a chair and slump down into it. "I guess you're right," she said. "I'm sorry for getting offended. I don't do well in high stress situations."

"I'm not sure any of us are doing perfectly in this situation," Simon said compassionately.

"We've got to keep our wits about us," Larry said. "The only way we get out of this is by thinking clearly and not jumping to rash conclusions."

"Or we simply wait for the lights to come back on," Coy said. "I don't like this talk of "the only way we get out of this." That sounds like we're all about to meet our doom."

"I think what he's trying to say is correct," Tobin said. "We all know there's a killer among us, or at least one on the loose. But unfortunately, we have no idea how long it might take for the power to come back up."

"What do you suggest we do in the meantime?" Coy asked. "We can't just stay here staring at each other all night."

"I think that's exactly what we should do," Tobin said. "Two of us need to remain awake at all times. For one thing, we need to lookout for each other, and for another, we need to keep each other honest."

"I don't understand." Delana shook her head. "What do you want us to do?"

"I'm saying we need to get some sleep," Tobin said. "But we need sentries. Two people to go on watch. I think one of the caterers should remain awake along with one of us. We don't know each other and that's more likely for us to keep each other honest."

"I'll start," Levi said. "I'll take the first watch." He tapped his flashlight against his thigh.

"Thank you for volunteering," Tobin said. "Who else? Who else wants to stay up and keep an eye out?"

"I'll do it," Larry said. "Not that I don't trust you buddy, but I'd feel better staying awake instead of falling asleep hoping nothing happens."

"No offense taken," Levi said. "I think we should make our rounds but stick to the Great Hall."

"I'll take that end," Larry said, pointing his flashlight toward the back of the room.

"I suppose I'll take the other end," Levi said, nodding.

"What are the rest of us supposed to do?" Delana asked. "I don't think I can sleep in here."

"You should try," Simon said. "We can put some of the cushions from the chairs on the floor."

"There's a stack of linen in every sideboard you see," Tobin said. "We can use the cushions as pallets and the linens as covers."

"Should we stick together in a group, or spread out?" Simon asked.

"I think I'd feel better sleeping next to my cousin," Marissa said.

"That's a good idea," Tobin said. "We can split up into small groups. That way the sentries have a better chance to keep an eye on us individually. Let's get started."

SIX

Carolina watched as Levi headed toward the far end of the Great Hall. She took Marissa by the hand again and led her to the sideboard closest to where he stood. Initially, she thought they might try to sleep just outside the entrance that led to the kitchen stairwell but decided against it. She wanted to be close to Levi more than anything.

By the candlelight, she could see the others follow suit. Delana took to the center of the room alone. Larry and Simon remained together and spread cushions on the floor just a few feet from each other. Tobin wasn't far off. Coy chose a spot closest to her, but still more than fifty feet away.

Marissa carefully removed several long tablecloths from the sideboard. She folded the first over the small bed of cushions she'd made. She spread another large cloth over the top, then handed a smaller cloth to Carolina. "We can cover up with these," she said.

"I don't know if I can get any sleep," Carolina whispered.

"Me either," Marissa said. "But I think we should try. Levi is close by, and he won't let anything happen to us."

"Are you guys alright down there?" Larry called out. "Maybe all you women should stick together."

"I'm just fine right where I'm at, thank you," Delana called back.

"I guess that's settled," Larry replied in a huff.

"She seems to have a chip on her shoulder," Marissa whispered to Carolina.

"I noticed that." Carolina lowered herself carefully to her knees. She crawled to the middle of the pallet and turned over on her back. She spread the tablecloth over herself and sighed. "It's hard to get comfortable."

"I know, but it's better than the floor," Marissa said.

"I don't like it," Delana said suddenly.

"You don't like what, exactly?" Tobin asked. Carolina could hear an edge of agitation in his voice.

"I don't like people whispering together," Delana said. She raised herself up and glared toward them. "These two down here keep talking to each other."

"Oh, leave them alone," Larry said. He didn't hide his agitation, unlike Tobin. "You heard them say they're cousins. I'm sure they're concerned, just like the rest of us. We all need to be quiet and go to sleep."

"I agree," Simon said. "We all need to just calm down and try to get some rest. Soon, the sun will be out, and we'll be able to see better. Hopefully, the lights will be up soon, too."

"Yeah, and then this nightmare will be over," Coy said.

"We'll settle down," Carolina called out. "And to answer your question, yes. Marissa is my younger cousin. We tend to look out for each other."

"Let's have silence now, then," Tobin said.

Carolina tried to close her eyes, but the flickering light was visible even with her eyelids pinched shut. She opened her eyes again and stared at the strange formations dancing across the high ceiling. The flickering candlelight painted airy pictures high above her head. A strange silence fell over them. She could hear the tick, tick, ticking of the wind-up clocks in the hallway outside the large room. What she couldn't hear were voices, or human sounds of any kind. She wondered where Bronson's many staff members had gone to, and if Darien was with them.

Most of all, she wondered who had killed Bronson and why.

Carolina rolled closer to her cousin. She felt Marissa's abdomen rise and fall, indicating she had fallen asleep. She closed her eyes and tried to slip away, but sleep never came. She could hear the men clearing their throats, walking back and forth, and venturing out into the corridors around the enormous room. In the silence, she realized that everything in the large room reverberated and echoed. Small sounds amplified into larger sounds.

Not knowing how long she had been lying there, Carolina rose at last while Marissa continued to sleep. She stretched her arms above her head and yawned, then glanced around the room. In the soft candlelight, she spotted Tobin and Simon speaking with their heads bowed close together at the other end of the room. Levi walked around the exterior, then came back through the doorway.

"Can't sleep?" he whispered when he joined her.

"Not exactly," Carolina said. "I need to use the restroom."

"I have no idea where the closest one is," Levi said.

"I'd better go ask Tobin, then."

"Do you want me to go with you?"

"No, you better stay here and keep watch," Carolina said. She pried a candle loose from the closest candelabra and headed across the room toward Tobin. Her shoes clicked softly as she walked.

"That isn't a very good idea," Tobin said when she approached. He nodded toward the candle in her hand.

"I didn't want to take the entire thing," Carolina said. "At any rate, I came to ask you where the closest restroom might be."

"That's a very good question," Simon said.

"First, let's start by giving you one of these," Tobin said, handing over a small, single candle holder and taking the one she was holding. "Second, allow me to show you."

"You're going to escort this young lady to the restroom by yourself?" Simon asked.

"Do you have a better idea?" Tobin replied.

"Maybe you could tell her where it's at and let her find it on her own," Simon said.

"Now, that wouldn't be very chivalrous of me, now would it?" Tobin asked.

"Still, I'd feel a little better if someone else went with me," Carolina said. "I mean no offense by that but, as you said back in the library, there is a killer loose in this house."

DRIZZLED IN MURDER

"And we have no idea who it might be," Simon said.

"Fine, then," Tobin said. "If you want to find your way to the bathroom by yourself, head out through the main entrance, and turn left toward the kitchen stairwell. Go past that and there will be a door to your right about ten meters down the hall."

"And is that the restroom?" Carolina asked.

"That will be the entrance to the housekeeper's office," Tobin continued. "Similar to your chambers, you will find a restroom behind one of the doors."

"You can't give her any more specific directions than that?" Simon asked.

"I'm afraid that's all there is," Tobin said. "Unless you want to traverse the stairwell by yourself, of course. There are bathrooms adjoining the kitchen."

"I'll think I'll take my chances down the hall," Carolina said.

"Would you like me to accompany you?" Simon asked. "Of course, I would invite another person along as well."

"Accompany her where?" Delana popped her head up and asked. She rose from her pallet and scurried

77

quickly across the floor to where they stood. "If she's going somewhere, I'm going as well."

"She's going to the restroom," Simon said. "Would you like to accompany us?"

"The restroom, yes," Delana said. Her tone lightened. "I have wondered where the facilities were located."

"Is there anyone else who would like to go as well?" Simon asked. He called across the room but kept his voice low enough so as not to disturb those who were already sleeping.

"Are you okay, Carolina?" Levi asked.

"I'll be fine," she said, then nodded to Simon.

"Ladies, if you'll follow me," Simon said, taking a bow. He picked up a candelabra and walked toward the back of the room, where Levi was keeping watch.

Carolina stuck close to Simon. She gripped the single candle holder tightly in her hand as she walked. Delana walked beside her, hugging the other side of the corridor.

DRIZZLED IN MURDER

Ahead, Carolina heard the soft ticking of a clock. She held her candle up, hoping to read the time on the face of the grandfather clock.

"Are you trying to tell what time it is?" Simon asked. He stopped and turned to face her.

"I was hoping to get a general idea," Carolina said.

"I don't think that clock works." Simon held the candelabra in front of him and stood in front of the clock. "Unless it is six-thirty, the hands are broken."

"That seems weird, doesn't it?"

"Not really. Old stuff like this breaks all the time." Simon shrugged.

"Yeah, I guess," Carolina said, thinking about it for a moment. "It might be part of the mystery too. When I first met Bronson, he told me I might find some odd things that are all part of the ruse."

"Unfortunately, I think we're a little past a ruse," Simon said.

"Can we just shut up and make this a faster trip?" Delana complained. "Some of us would like to get back to sleep."

"Aren't you curious what time it is?" Simon asked.

"Yeah, doesn't it make you a little nervous having no idea how many hours we have left until daylight?" Carolina asked.

"Why would I care? I've got a watch back in my room if it really matters. All I know is that it's the middle of the night, we're stuck in this monstrous tomb, and my brother is missing."

"I'm sure we'll go looking for him in the morning," Carolina said, trying to sound reassuring. "It's just too difficult at night without the power on."

"Thank you for those wise words, Captain Obvious," Delana said.

Simon locked eyes with Carolina and shrugged. "I suppose we should get a move on," he said. They continued down the corridor until they reached the door on the right, as Tobin had described. Carolina hung back as Simon opened it and held on for a moment, searching for something to prop it open with.

"Delana, would you please take this?" he asked, holding the candelabra toward her.

DRIZZLED IN MURDER

"No way," Delana said. "Hold it yourself."

Carolina stepped forward and took the candelabra out of his hands while Simon found a small chair and leaned it against the door. She handed the candelabra back and ventured further into the chambers.

"I'm first," Delana said. She yanked the candle out of Carolina's hands and headed toward the door.

"She's pleasant," Simon whispered after the door had closed behind Delana.

"She's something," Carolina said quietly. She waited next to Simon. Flickering light from the candles cast an eerie glow over the large room. Carolina caught herself checking back toward the open door multiple times while they waited for Delana to finish. The sound of rushing water filled the room, then Delana exited the bathroom.

"Ladies first," Simon said. Carolina held her hand out to Delana for the candle.

"No way," Delana said, pulling her arm back. "This light is mine now."

"Miss Hart," Simon said. He handed his candelabra off to her. "Be careful with the flames." Carolina nodded and headed to the restroom. She set the candles on the vanity while she used the facilities, then quickly opened the door. The longer they were separated from the others, the more the cold chill crept down her back.

Carolina pulled the bathroom door open and reentered the office chamber. She was shocked to find the room empty. "Simon? Delana?" she called out. She gripped the heavy candelabra in her hand and made a circle around the room, opening the other doors as she went. Her two companions were nowhere in sight.

SEVEN

Carolina rushed back out into the hall. She stood for a second, trying to get her bearings. At last, she turned and headed back toward the kitchen stairwell. She breathed a little easier when she passed it, recognizing it as a landmark that told her she was close to the Great Hall. Along the way, she looked back over her shoulder for any sign of the single candle Delana had been holding.

"Where are the others?" Tobin asked as soon as Carolina entered the large room.

"You mean they didn't come back here?" She set the candelabra on the nearest table and rubbed her shoulder. The weight of the large brass candle holder had taken a toll on her joints.

"No, they didn't come back here," Tobin said.

Larry rose from his pallet on the floor, standing quickly. "You mean to say they left you?"

"Simon handed me the candles, so I could use the restroom," Carolina explained. "Delana had taken my candle from me previously. When I opened the bathroom door, the room was empty. They were gone."

"Did they say a word to you about where they were headed?" Tobin asked.

"No, they didn't say a thing," Carolina said. "All we really talked about was what time it was. It seemed like all the clocks were broken, which we thought was kind of strange."

"Yeah, yeah." Tobin waved it off. "That was part of the murder mystery but, how sure are you that the room was empty?"

"Did you hear them arguing? Were they in a hurry?" Larry asked before she had a chance to reply.

"I heard nothing," Carolina said. "Absolutely nothing. I was shocked when I opened the door."

"There are three other rooms that attach to that chamber," Tobin said.

"I made my way around and looked in each," Carolina said. "I mean, I suppose they could have been in a closet or something but that wouldn't make a whole lot of sense."

"I'm sure you would have heard them had they opened the door," Tobin said. He dropped his chin to his chest and shook his head. "Two more people roaming around the castle is just what we need."

"Do you think, I mean, is it possible, that one of them was intent on hurting the other?" Larry asked.

"I don't know," Carolina said. "I just don't know. I have no idea where they went."

"What's going on?" Levi asked, rushing to her side from the other end of the Great Hall.

"Simon and Delana have gone missing," Tobin said.

"Are you alright, Carolina?" Levi asked.

"I'm fine, just a little shaken."

"I heard voices," Coy said, rousing from his nap. "What's happening now?"

"Three of us went to the restroom," Carolina said. "Only, when I came back out again, the other two were gone."

"Gone, as in, they left the room?" Coy asked carefully.

"Yeah, yeah, they left the room," Carolina said. "No one else has passed away to my knowledge."

"But they weren't fighting?" Tobin asked again. "They weren't exchanging words or anything before you went to the restroom?"

"Delana was a little snippy," Carolina said. "But I get the feeling that's her default tone. Nothing unusual there."

"Should we go after them?" Levi asked.

"In a dark castle in the middle of the night," Coy said. "You want us to take off looking for two people who may or may not want to be found."

"What do you mean, they may or may not want to be found?" Carolina said.

"I mean, if they went off somewhere together, maybe they wanted to be alone," Coy said. "It isn't unheard of."

DRIZZLED IN MURDER

"Did they know each other?" Carolina asked.

"Honestly, I have no idea," Tobin said. "I didn't know anything about any of you until Bronson sprung this murder mystery weekend on me."

"How do you know Bronson?" Carolina asked.

"You wouldn't believe it, but we went to college together," Tobin said, shaking his head. "He was the strange, eccentric dude who knew how to live life. And I was the studious, silent loser."

"Based on your address, I wouldn't exactly call you the loser," Coy said, looking overhead.

"I have done very well for myself, yes," Tobin said. "But Bronson was always the one who knew how to live life and get the most out of it."

"And he surprised you with the idea of this murder mystery weekend without notice?" Levi asked.

"Essentially, yes," Tobin said. "He told me he wanted to visit me for the weekend, and then he announced that he was bringing some friends along with him."

"Maybe that's why he booked the catering gig last minute," Carolina said.

"He booked you last minute?" Tobin asked. "That must not have been part of the plan."

"Does he always travel with a staff of twelve or more?" Coy asked.

"Honestly, I'm not sure," Tobin said. "He simply told me he needed accommodations for his staff. I thought he meant a personal assistant. He explained just about everything to me, just not until after the fact."

"I still find it odd that we haven't heard from or seen any of those staff members," Levi said.

"What are you all talking about over here?" Larry asked, returning from a quick walk to the other side of the room.

"Bronson and his staff," Coy said. "Apparently, Tobin here didn't know anything about this murder mystery weekend until Bronson sprung it on him out of nowhere."

"That's odd," Larry said. "With a fellow like that, you'd expect to have his plans made months ahead of time."

"It surprises us, as well," Carolina said.

"I wonder if he's ever had any trouble before?" Tobin asked. "Maybe whoever killed him followed him here."

"I hope y'all are considering the obvious," Larry said.

"And what would that be?" Tobin asked.

"That one of his staff members had it out for him," Larry said. "And it would be the perfect cover, too,"

"Do you mean because of the storm?" Levi asked. "How could anyone predict the lights would go out?"

"That's not exactly what I mean," Larry said. "Look at how they dress. Can you tell them apart? Hats pulled down over their faces, the same shirt, pants, and shoes. Not to mention those weird aprons. It would be really hard to pick one out from a lineup."

"He has a point," Coy said.

"We still haven't officially decided if we should go after Delana and Simon or not," Levi said.

Tobin sighed. "The way I see it, we'd be better off waiting until first light."

"Hey, does anyone know what time it is?" Carolina said. "We tried to read the grandfather clock in the hall on the way to the bathroom, but the hands appeared to be malfunctioning."

"You know, when I think about it, it's odd that we haven't heard any of those great big clocks chiming on the hour," Larry said. "Are all your clocks electric?"

"No, they aren't," Tobin said. He glanced toward the corridor leading to the kitchen stairwell. "But now that you mention it, I haven't heard from one of them this whole evening."

"I'm not sure it even matters right now," Coy said. "I vote we get as much sleep as we possibly can. All of us."

"What about the lookouts?" Larry asked. "Don't you think we need to keep our eyes out?"

"For what, exactly?" Coy asked. "You guys said there's a killer on the loose in the castle. What are the chances he can find his way back here? What we need is rest."

"And after that, we're going to need nourishment," Tobin said. "Do you think your crew can prepare

DRIZZLED IN MURDER

something to eat in the morning?"

"Of course we can," Carolina said. "Although, it may not be as gourmet as we expected. Especially if the lights haven't come back on."

"We'll do our very best," Levi said.

"I don't care what it is," Tobin said. "Even if the power isn't back on, we're still going to need refreshment."

Levi followed Carolina back to the small pallet where Marissa was sleeping. She settled down next to her cousin while Levi removed a few more cushions and made room for himself above their heads. "Just do your best to get some rest," he whispered in the dark. "We need to get as much rest as possible."

"Surely the power will be back on in the morning," Carolina said. "Don't you think so?"

"I honestly have no idea," Levi said. Carolina watched the strained look on his face in the candlelight. "I have a feeling we're not going to like what the morning reveals."

"What do you mean by that?" Marissa whispered.

"Oh, I didn't know you were awake," Carolina said.

"I've been awake for a little while."

"Then why didn't you say something?" Carolina asked.

"I was just trying to lay here and listen," Marissa said. "I wanted to see if I could hear something while everyone was talking."

"Hear something like what?" Levi asked.

"Footsteps, noises around the castle," Marissa said.

"And? Did you hear anything?" Carolina asked.

"Nothing of importance," Marissa said. She opened her eyes and looked up. "You go ahead and get some sleep, Levi. I've been resting long enough, so I think I can stay awake. I promise I'll shake you if I hear anything."

"Are you sure?" Levi asked.

"I'm positive."

Levi nodded. "But if you hear anything, you don't hesitate to get me up. Alright?"

"You got it," Marissa said. Carolina smiled at her cousin and turned to face the other wall.

EIGHT

"Carolina," Marissa's voice penetrated her thoughts. She felt pressure on her shoulder. "Carolina. Wake up."

Carolina rolled over and blinked until her eyes focused on the light and the room. She sat up quickly and looked around. Light streamed into the room from the various corridors. "What time is it?" she asked.

"Probably just before six," Levi said. She turned to find him sitting upright on his bed of cushions. "Are you ready to head downstairs?"

"I'm ready," Marissa said. "First thing I want to do is look for coffee."

"Is the power back on?" Carolina asked.

"Not that we can tell," Levi said.

"What about the others?" Carolina asked. "Is anyone else up?"

"I haven't seen anyone else move," Marissa said.

"Have you seen or heard from Simon and Delana?" Carolina asked. She searched Marissa's face.

"I'm afraid not," Marissa said. "Come on, let's go." She stood and held out her hand. Carolina took it and allowed her cousin to help her to her feet.

"Let's get downstairs and get busy," Levi whispered as they walked toward the corridor. "The busier we are, the quicker time will pass."

"I hope you're right," Carolina said. She followed Marissa down the hall and stopped just outside of the kitchen stairwell. Levi pulled the door open and stopped.

"We need to be careful," he said.

"What's going on?" Carolina asked.

"Oh, nothing," Levi said, smiling quickly. "It's just that the stairs are dark still. There isn't a lot of natural light until you get to the bottom." He held out his hand for Carolina. Marissa brought up the rear, grabbing onto Carolina's shirt.

Slowly, they made their way down the stairs. Carolina held tight to Levi with one hand and the handrail with the other. The sound of their footsteps filled the narrow space. She could see the light at the bottom of the spiral stairs. About halfway down, Levi stopped.

"Did you hear that?" he whispered.

"Hear what?" Marissa asked.

"Listen," Levi said. They stood stock-still for a moment. Carolina closed her eyes and strained to listen. In the distance, she could hear the tap, tap, tap of steps high above them.

"I bet that's Bronson's staff," Marissa said.

"I bet you're right," Carolina said. They continued down the steps toward the kitchen.

"I wonder if they know," Marissa asked as they made their way through the arched entrance into the kitchen.

"You mean about Bronson?" Levi asked. "I don't know, but it might be telling if they do."

"Because they wouldn't have heard unless..." Marissa said.

"Unless one of them is the killer," Carolina said, finishing the sentence for her.

"Who do you think did this?" Marissa asked, gazing at Carolina.

"I have no idea," Carolina said.

"Not even a little bit of an idea?" Marissa asked. "Nothing seems suspicious to you?"

"That's the problem," Carolina said. "Everything and everyone seems suspicious to me. Any of the ones who found Bronson's body is a potential killer. Tobin himself could be the one. And then there's Simon and Delana who both disappeared last night."

"Not to mention Delana's brother," Marissa said.

"I just hope we don't find any more like Bronson," Levi muttered.

"Look, you guys were right before," Carolina said. "We need to be busy. I don't know how we're going to cook, though."

"I do," Levi said. He headed for one of the ancient cast iron stoves pushed against the wall. "Did you see the stack of wood underneath?" he asked. He pointed to a tidy stack of split wood that lined the kitchen wall.

"You're not going to cook on that, are you?" Marissa asked.

"Do you have a better solution?" Levi asked, smiling. "Besides, I saw some cast iron skillets hanging above the fireplace. I'm sure we can whip up some eggs in no time."

"That sounds good to me," Carolina said.

"Does that mean we have to go down to the pantry?" Marissa asked.

"I think we can find everything in the refrigerators up here," Levi said.

"But won't the eggs be bad?" Marissa asked.

"Not for a while yet. Although, we shouldn't stand with the refrigerator door open any longer than necessary," Levi said as he quickly retrieved the eggs.

"I'm going to check this one as well," Carolina said, opening the refrigerator closest to her. She was surprised to see ham steaks on one of the shelves. "I suppose it won't matter if we use these." She opened the crisper door and retrieved several onions, green peppers, and other vegetables.

Levi got to work adding several pieces of wood to the belly of one of the cast iron stoves. He searched around the cupboards until he located a box of matches. Within minutes, a fire roared to life.

"What can I do to help?" Marissa asked.

"I could sure use some help with prep work," Levi said. He located a large bowl and handed it to Marissa.

While Marissa cracked and whipped the eggs, Carolina began cutting up vegetables. She cubed potatoes, then rinsed them and patted them dry. Levi added oil to each of the pans while Carolina carefully placed the potatoes in the oil. She turned and placed her hands on her hips, searching around the kitchen.

"Look over there," she said, pointing to a small cupboard on the other side of the large room. "I think I see the makings of some biscuits."

"I'll take over the potatoes," Marissa announced.

Carolina located another large bowl and began adding white flour by the cup. She measured out the baking powder, salt, and a little sugar then carefully stirred it together. After another quick search, she found a type of shortening and cut it in. She returned to the fridge she had pulled the ham steaks from and found a carton of milk. "Might as well use this up," she said.

"I'd say we've got quite a feast here," Levi announced a short time later.

Carolina stood at one of the long tables, carefully removing hot biscuits onto a platter. "I wonder if there's enough here for the staff as well."

"There should be," Levi said. "Although I wonder when we'll actually hear from them."

"I'm not in any hurry to go exploring any dark corridors of this castle," Marissa said. "Hopefully they just smell the food and come to us."

"I wonder if we'll see Simon or Delana today," Levi said.

"Or Darien," Carolina added. "This whole situation is just so strange. Who would have ever thought the murder mystery weekend would turn out to be a real thing?"

"I wonder if Simon is right," Marissa said. "Do you think it's possible that this is just some weird, sick ruse?"

"I don't think so," Carolina said. "I checked that man's body. And unless that was a very good fake, Bronson is dead."

"The question is who would want to kill him," Marissa said.

"I have my suspicions," Levi said.

"You can't just say that and not elaborate," Marissa said. "Go on. Spill it. Who do you think did this?"

"Well, for starters, I think Darien is a very good suspect."

DRIZZLED IN MURDER

"Based on what, exactly?" Carolina asked.

"Based on the fact that he's been missing in action since this began," Levi said. "He has been skulking around this castle in the dark. That alone makes me suspicious."

"But what would his motive be?" Marissa asked.

"I don't think we know enough about any of these people to guess a motive," Carolina said. "Unless, well... Never mind."

"Oh, no," Levi said. "If I had to spill the beans, so do you. What were you going to say?"

"I was going to say that I think Tobin himself might be a good suspect," Carolina said. "You heard him. He's known Bronson since they were in college together. I don't know about you, but I detected a little bit of jealousy in his voice when he described them back when they were in school."

"I'm not sure I picked up on that," Marissa said.

"It wasn't blatant or anything," Carolina said. "It was more something in his voice when he described himself as a studious loser and Bronson as the weird guy who always had fun. There was something about the way he said it that made me wonder."

"But would you have had those thoughts if Bronson hadn't wound up dead?" Levi asked. "It might be possible that you read jealousy into his description because of Bronson's murder."

"That's true," Carolina admitted. "What about Simon? Do you think it's possible he's the killer?"

"Based on what motive?" Levi asked.

"Again, I'm not sure about a motive," Carolina said. "But I do think it's weird that he disappeared with Delana. And there was something else."

"What?" Marissa said. "You have to stop leaving me in suspense here."

"I don't know if it means anything at all," Carolina said. "But I thought it was weird that Simon noticed the clock in the hall. I looked for the time, but he told me he thought the other clocks had been disabled, too."

"He is an actor, after all," Levi said. "Maybe he's just trained to be observant."

"Maybe," Carolina said. "Even so. I just thought it was weird."

"And then there's Delana," Marissa said.

"You think Delana is the killer?" Carolina looked up from the platter of biscuits at her cousin.

"No, I just think she's a really nasty person," Marissa said. "And she was one of the first people to discover Bronson's body. She was the one who screamed."

"The fact that she screamed would indicate that she was shocked at the discovery of his body, though," Levi said.

"Unless that was an act to throw everyone else off," Carolina said.

"Great, we're back to square one," Marissa said. "And we haven't even begun to talk about members of Bronson's staff."

NINE

Carolina followed Levi back up the steps toward the Great Hall. She balanced the platter of biscuits on her arms. The heat rose to her face, causing her to feel lightheaded as she trudged up the steep staircase. Marissa followed behind, carrying a large urn filled with hot coffee.

"I thought I smelled something wafting from downstairs," Coy exclaimed as they walked into the Great Hall with the feast.

"What are we supposed to do for plates and silverware?" Larry asked.

"Don't worry about that," Tobin said. He moved to the buffet sideboard where he'd found the candelabras the night before. "I have flatware and dishes in almost every large area of the castle. That and candlesticks, of course." He produced a stack of plates and a handful of forks, then turned around to smile at the crowd when he found a few mugs for their coffee.

"I can't believe you made this without any electricity," Coy said, helping himself to three of the hot biscuits.

"Slow down there," Levi said. "We don't know if the others are going to join us or not."

"What others?" Tobin asked.

"Simon, Delana, and Darien, for starters," Levi said.

"Not to mention all of Bronson's staff members," Carolina said. She picked up a single biscuit and topped it with a small section of ham steak and a spoonful of eggs.

They ate quickly, leaving about half of the food for any others who might venture into the hall. Tobin suggested they return to the kitchen with the leftovers.

Carolina began gathering up the fragments of their breakfast. She loaded a platter with dirty dishes and headed for the large entrance near the kitchen stairwell. She was halfway there when another curdling blood scream rang out through a nearby corridor. Instantly, she dropped the platter. Dishes clattered to the floor. Several coffee mugs shattered on the stone beneath her feet.

Carolina turned back, eyes wild, and searched the faces of the others. "Where did that come from?" she gasped.

"I'm not sure," Tobin said. His face had gone pale. "I think it was that way." He pointed down the hall toward the office chamber where Carolina had used the restroom the night before.

"We have to go check it out," Coy said. "We have to go see."

"Don't worry about the mess," Tobin commanded. "Let's go together. All of us."

Tobin headed for the entryway, stopping at another sideboard along the way. He pulled a drawer open and retrieved several brass candlesticks, passing them out to the others.

"What is this for?" Levi asked.

"We don't know what we're going to find," Tobin said. "We are all in danger here. We might as well go armed with something."

"Let's get this over with," Larry barked. Carolina glanced over her shoulder at the older man. Beads of sweat had formed along his brow. He pulled a linen handkerchief from his pocket and dabbed his face.

Together, they walked slowly down the hall. Carolina glanced in the office chamber as they passed the open door. They practically huddled together as they walked. Tobin led the group toward the sunshine which gleamed through the windows at the end of the hall. Carolina braced herself for a discovery when they rounded a corner and entered another large, cavernous room.

"What's going on here?" Tobin demanded. Carolina forced herself to look. She was shocked to see several individuals, all dressed differently.

"Are these the staff members?" Coy asked. He raised his head and spoke louder. "Are you all members of Bronson's staff?"

DRIZZLED IN MURDER

It was difficult to tell because of the lack of similar uniforms. Carolina scanned the faces. They stood in a group, surrounding something or someone.

"Yeah, we work for Bronson," a young woman said. "My name is Kelly. I'm the head of this group. We've got some of your friends here."

The group of staff members stepped away. Once again, Carolina braced herself to see a body on the floor. But she was shocked to find Simon, Delana, and her brother Darien seated on the floor.

"What is going on here?" Tobin demanded again.

"We were just having a conversation," Kelly said. "And these people claimed our boss was killed last night. That was a shock to some of us, hence the screaming. Is that true? Is Bronson dead?"

Carolina glanced at Levi. He looked up at the large chandelier hanging in the middle of the room, as if willing the power to come back on. No one spoke for a moment.

"Come on," Delana said, rising slowly to her feet. "Tell these people what happened. They don't seem to believe me."

"She's right," Larry said finally. "Several of us were together and we heard screaming. That's when we found Bronson laying on the floor of the library, dead as a doornail."

"You can't be serious," Kelly said. There was a collective gasp among her other staff members. "What happened? Was he murdered?"

"We might want to ask you all that same question," Tobin said.

"None of us did a thing to him," Kelly said. Carolina studied her face as she spoke, eager to spot any clue that might indicate whether she was telling the truth or not.

"How did you all come to work for Bronson?" Carolina asked.

"Who cares?" Delana snapped. "All I care about is getting the heck out of here. Right now, Tobin. You have to let us out of here."

"I'm not keeping you here," Tobin said. "I explained to you last night that it is a result of the alarm system."

"An alarm system you installed," Delana said.

DRIZZLED IN MURDER

"Maybe we should hear from Bronson's employees," Coy suggested.

"Scholarships," Kelly said. "Each one of us was awarded a scholarship from Bronson. A full ride to college. We worked for him through the summer. It's one of the stipulations."

"Does that make any of you upset?" Marissa asked. "That you have to work for him in the summer?"

"Absolutely not," Kelly said. "Bronson awarded scholarships to people who don't normally qualify for them." She looked around the room. "None of us are perfect students, but he gave us a chance. If you don't believe me, look on his website. There's a bio for each of us. It tells the story." Her words were followed by several murmurs from her coworkers, and verifying what she said was true.

"Why are you holding these people here?" Tobin asked.

"They were just asking questions," Simon said, standing up. "They found us wandering around this morning and confronted us about what was going on."

111

"He's right." Kelly nodded. "All the clocks aren't working for some reason, so we went off trying to figure out what time it was. That's when we found them."

"Where did you go last night?" Carolina asked. "You and Delana just took off when I was in the bathroom."

"They came looking for me," Darien said. "At least, my sister did. I'm not sure what that guy was doing."

"Delana insisted upon going into the deep of this castle in search of her brother," Simon said. He shook his head. "I just went after her. I didn't want anyone else winding up dead like Bronson."

"You're lucky nothing happened to you," Larry scolded.

"And I specifically remember asking everyone to stick together," Tobin said.

"What about the rest of you?" Levi asked. "What were you doing all night?"

"Honestly, sleeping," Kelly said with a shrug. "We were exhausted."

DRIZZLED IN MURDER

"Exhausted from what?" Coy said. "The so-called murder mystery weekend wasn't even supposed to start until today."

"Maybe not for the rest of you," Kelly said. "But we had to scrub this entire place floor to ceiling."

"Tell me," Carolina interrupted. "Did you all help set up the murder mystery aspect of this weekend?"

"Oh, yes. We handle every last detail when it comes to the mystery. It's partly why we distance ourselves from the guests. Bronson never wanted us to be swayed to give any clues."

"That's enough," Tobin said suddenly. "I'm exhausted. Now that it's daylight, I would like to return to my own living quarters."

"Wait a second," Coy said. "I thought you wanted us to stick together."

"That is what you said," Larry agreed.

"And that's what we've been doing," Tobin said. "Since eleven o'clock last night, we have done nothing but stick together, and you see where it's gotten us. I'm going to my room. It isn't like we're going to suddenly discover who the killer is. My suggestion is you all stick together in groups. Wait it out until the power comes back on, then leave this place at once and forget you ever knew it existed."

Carolina glanced around the room. Unlike the Great Hall, she was surprised to see the room was actually a very large sitting room. Wingback chairs grouped in numbers of four dotted the expanse of space. Two large fireplaces bookended the interior walls of the room. The outside wall was nearly all glass.

Tobin turned on his heel and began to walk toward the corridor. He passed another grandfather style clock. Carolina released her grip on Levi's arm and followed him a few steps. She stopped when the clock's face came into view. "We don't need to wait," she blurted out. Tobin stopped and turned to face her.

"What are you going on about?" he asked, his eyebrows drew together in frustration.

"To find out who the killer is," she said. "We don't have to wait. He's right here with us."

"This is ridiculous," Tobin said. "I've had it up to here with you people being in my house. I'm headed

DRIZZLED IN MURDER

to bed. If you think you know who the killer is, tell it to the others."

"Carolina, what are you doing?" Levi joined her suddenly and whispered in her ear.

"Putting things together, that's what I'm doing," Carolina said. Her heart raced in her chest. She felt the fatigue of the past day weighing down on her, but she pressed on. "It was you, Mr. Crutchfield."

"I beg your pardon," Tobin said, stopping again.

"Delana, were you alone when you discovered Bronson's body last night in the library?" Carolina asked, turning to the angry woman.

"Yeah, I was by myself," Delana said. "I was in the corridor outside of the library when the lights went out."

"But you happened to have a flashlight with you?" Larry asked.

"Of course I did. A woman always comes prepared," Delana said. "I was looking for Darien. He took off shortly after dinner. I wanted to find him before he got into some sort of trouble."

"Is that true, Darian?" Carolina asked. "Did you just take off?"

"Yeah, she's telling the truth," Darien said, blushing. "I don't like crowds. I didn't want to be here."

"Then why did you come?" Simon asked.

"Because I was made to come," Darien said. "I used to be one of you." He pointed at Kelly and the others. "I worked for Bronson for several summers while I was in college. Only, I dropped out and never heard the end of it. This weekend I planned to make it up to him."

"That sounds like motive to kill," Tobin said, suddenly excited. He grinned widely and pointed toward Darien. "There you go. There's your killer."

"He's not the killer," Kelly said. "I told you that we went to sleep last night. Well, Darien was out here with us."

"You were with them the whole time?" Delana asked.

"We played cards, passed around a couple of bottles of whiskey," Darien said.

DRIZZLED IN MURDER

"I thought you didn't want to be around people," Delana said.

"Clearly that's not true," Larry said. "How many of you would testify that Darien was with you all night?" He directed his question at the group of young staff members.

"Looks like it's unanimous," Simon said, nodding to Kelly and her coworkers. Each one raised a hand high above their heads.

"This proves nothing at all," Tobin said.

"Maybe not," Carolina said. "But there are other things that do."

"Like what, exactly?" Coy asked.

"Like the clocks," Carolina said. She pointed to the grandfather clock in the corridor close to Tobin. "I must admit, Simon. I was suspicious of you for a while last night."

"Suspicious of me? Why on earth would you be suspicious of me?" Simon asked.

"When I tried to find the time on the clock in the hallway last night, you said all of the clocks were that way in the castle," Carolina explained. "Somehow, you noticed that each of the clocks had stopped working. I thought it was odd."

"And now? You don't suspect him anymore?" Coy asked.

"No, I do not," Carolina said. She turned her gaze back to Tobin. "But there was something else."

"This is so far past ridiculous," Tobin said. "I can't believe I'm still standing here."

"Why don't you just stay right where you are," Larry said. "This is something we all need to hear."

"It was the candlesticks," Carolina said. "That part took even longer for me to put together. Bronson died after he was hit over the head with a candlestick. Earlier, in the Great Hall, Tobin, you explained at breakfast that there are dishes and cutlery in nearly every large space in the castle. But last night you also said there were candlesticks everywhere. That's how you killed him."

"That proves absolutely nothing," Tobin roared. "Here I thought Bronson was the only one out of his mind. But clearly, he has assembled a cast of characters equally as insane as he was." He took off walking at a fast speed.

"Was that the only reason?" Larry whispered when Tobin was out of ear shot. "Is that the only clue you have?"

Carolina shook her head. "Didn't you hear him a little while ago? He said we have been going at this since eleven o'clock last night."

"But the clocks had been stopped," Simon said.

"Exactly," Carolina said. "Tobin is the only one who knew what time this whole nightmare began. At first, Tobin said the clocks not working was part of the weekend, but then we got confirmation that Bronson's staff thought the clocks were broken, which means it wasn't part of the weekend after all. Tobin messed with things to scare us. When people don't feel like they have any control, it's much easier to keep them confused. We were arguing about everything and not working together. Losing knowledge about simple things, like what time it was, combined with it being dark... well, it just kept us all off our toes."

TEN

"Well, how was it?" Uncle Toad asked when Carolina and the others walked through the back door to the Hart Family Restaurant.

"Don't ask," Marissa said. She slumped down in Carolina's chair and laid her head on the desk in front of her.

"That bad, huh?" Uncle Toad chuckled. "Well, you might as well go home and get some rest."

"Aren't you going to even ask why we're here in the middle of the day on Saturday afternoon?" Carolina asked.

"I don't have to ask," Uncle Toad said. "I heard everything. It was all over the news."

"It was? You heard about what happened at the castle?" Levi asked. Marissa picked her head back up off the desk.

"Millionaire Tobin Crutchfield was arrested for the murder of his longtime friend, Bronson Declue, during a murder mystery weekend at the famed Bonneville Castle," Uncle Toad said. "Something like that, anyway. Tell me, how long were the lights out?"

"Too long," Marissa said.

"The lights came back up right after Carolina declared Tobin was the killer," Levi said, beaming proudly.

"Of course they did," Uncle Toad said, nodding.

"What do you mean, of course they did?" Carolina asked. Irritation stewed in her. She was too keyed up to give even Uncle Toad a pass for teasing her.

"I mean, it's just your luck the lights would come back on then," Uncle Toad said, smiling. "I also meant it was no surprise to me that you were the one to figured out who killed Bronson."

"What makes you say that?" Marissa asked.

DRIZZLED IN MURDER

"Oh, that's an easy one," Denise said, sailing into the storage room.

"Good to see you too," Carolina snapped.

"Oh, yeah. Welcome back, you guys," Denise said. "And I was serious. It's no surprise to any of us when you figure out these things, Carolina."

"Where are you going with this?" Carolina asked.

"Face it," Denise said. "You guys have run into more weird situations than anybody I know. And, well, you may be a woman of many talents, but you're also a gifted detective, Carolina."

"I am not," Carolina said, eager to argue with anyone over any point of view. "Right now, I am a tired business owner who wants nothing more than a bubble bath and a warm bed."

"She's got a point," Uncle Toad said. "How did you know this Tobin guy was the killer?"

"She figured it out because he was the only one who knew what time it was when the body was discovered last night," Marissa said. "She also said something about candlesticks."

"Candlesticks? What does that have to do with anything?" Denise asked.

"The killer used a candlestick," Levi said quickly.

"Of course he did," Denise said. "That proves my point right there. Only you would have figured that out, Carolina. I bet you figured out the motive, too."

"The motive was simple," Carolina said. "All you had to do was listen to him for more than five minutes. He told us everything when he described how Bronson had surprised him with the idea of a murder mystery weekend."

"See? Only Carolina could have figured that out," Denise said.

"Watch it, Denise," Marissa said. "The rest of us had pretty good theories going, too."

"I'm sure you did," Denise said. "That makes you all a good team, but it's usually Carolina who figures everything out in the end."

"Are you saying I should quit catering altogether?" Carolina asked. "Because if you suggest I open some sort of weird detective agency, I'm going to throw a can of tomatoes at you."

DRIZZLED IN MURDER

"I wouldn't suggest that," Denise said. "I don't think you have the patience to run a detective agency, but I do think you're good at it."

"Who even runs a detective agency anymore?" Marissa asked. She returned to the chair and plopped down on it. "That sounds like something from a cartoon."

"There are still private detectives," Levi said. "Although I do agree. You really ought to stick to catering for now, Carolina."

"After this weekend, I'm not sure I ever want to cater another event again, never mind anything else," Carolina said.

"Oh, you shouldn't give up on catering altogether," Uncle Toad said. "Although I would pass on the next job that takes place in an old castle."

AUTHOR'S NOTE

I'd love to hear your thoughts on my books, the storylines, and anything else that you'd like to comment on—reader feedback is very important to me. My contact information, along with some other helpful links, is listed on the next page. If you'd like to be on my list of "folks to contact" with updates, release and sales notifications, etc.... just shoot me an email and let me know. Thanks for reading!

Also...

... if you're looking for more great reads, Summer Prescott Books publishes several popular series by outstanding Cozy Mystery authors.

CONTACT SUMMER PRESCOTT
BOOKS PUBLISHING

Blog and Book Catalog: http://summerprescottbooks.com

Email: summer.prescott.cozies@gmail.com

And...be sure to check out the Summer Prescott Cozy Mysteries fan page and Summer Prescott Books Publishing Page on Facebook – let's be friends!

To sign up for our fun and exciting newsletter, which will give you opportunities to win prizes and swag, enter contests, and be the first to know about New Releases, click here: http://summerprescottbooks.com

Made in United States
North Haven, CT
11 August 2025

71566940R00080